D1413382

HEAD

LACROSSE GOALIE

CASE

Sports Fiction with a Winning Edge

bright sky press

2365 Rice Blvd., Suite 202 Houston, Texas 77005

10   9   8   7   6   5   4   3   2

Library of Congress Cataloging-in-Publication Data

Chambers, Sam T.
Head case : lacrosse goalie / Sam T. Chambers and Dr. Bob Rotella.
p. cm. — (Sports fiction with a winning edge ;
1) Summary: Although younger and smaller, fifth-grader Max is chosen to be the starting goalie for a local lacrosse league, but his lack of confidence drives him to train to the point of obsesssion until he receives help from a sports psychologist.
ISBN 978-1-933979-40-3 (pbk.)
[1. Lacrosse—Fiction. 2. Self-confidence—Fiction. 3. Sports—Psychological aspects—Fiction.]
I. Rotella, Robert J. II. Title. III. Series.

PZ7.C35736He 2009
[Fic]—dc22
                                2009016617

Book and cover design by Cregan Design
Illustrations by Don Collins
Edited by Stephanie Wiegand
Printed in Canada through Friesens

HEAD

LACROSSE GOALIE

CASE

Sports Fiction with a Winning Edge

Sam T. Chambers
& Dr. Bob Rotella

Illustrations by Don Collins

bright sky press
HOUSTON, TEXAS

Dedication

To Rodney Rullman, Jay Stalfort, Ben O'Neal, Duffy Birkhead, Sabu, Ed Williams, Hunter Francis, Doug Sarant, Stephen Devlin, Dan Shavitz, Brad Harper, Calvin Tsao, Charlie Gramatges, Philip Meicler, Jason Grasty, Giorgio Angelini, Jacob Robinson, Ernst Leiss, Ben May, David Atlas, Kevin Dowlen, Jeremy Slawin, Henry Waller, Krishnan Rajagopalan, Nick Tutcher, Jack McDaniel, Grant Williams, Boone Bajgier, Nate Whittle, Gabe Louis, Harrison Proffitt, William Trieschman, and Zach Coton

who taught me what happens between the pipes.

-STC

Table of Contents

Chapter One

Max Speyer lifted his big goalie stick over his head and felt his gloves settle over his hands. He looked through the bars of his helmet and saw the Powhatans, the select team he had dreamed of joining since he first picked up a lacrosse stick at age six, spread out beyond the crease. Here he was, actually starting in goal. But somehow, now that he had finally made the team, his dream was taking a wrong turn. Past the fourth quarter horn, the Powhatans were three minutes deep in the agony of overtime.

Chris and Reeves, two sixth grade Powhatan attackmen Max didn't know well, worked the ball toward the Algonquin goal. Max wanted the Powhatans to score and win in sudden victory. Just as badly, though, he wanted to get some action

7

down in the defense to prove to Coach Rollman he had made the right decision in picking Max over Cheese Dog to start in goal. Max had practiced his technique every day since he came home from goalie camp last summer, and he was ready to shine.

A Powhatan shot bounced in the dust in front of the opposite goal, and the Algonquin goalie glided to block it high in the top right corner of the goal.

"Lucky grab," thought Max, as he watched the other goalie loft the ball toward midfield. Johnny Bonner, the Algonquin's best attackman, nabbed it. Max, and everybody else in the league, knew Bonner. He had cheetah speed, a deceptive stick, and the intimidating nickname, "Snake Eyes."

Max bobbed on his toes and twitched his fingers in his gloves. "Come on Bonner, bring it on," he muttered to himself. At ten, Max was the youngest starting goalie to ever play for the Powhatans, and he wanted to be the one to stop Snake Eyes. He had played in goal since he was six, he regularly studied every play in the Bob Scott book his dad had given him as soon as he could read, and he had gone to Bill Pilat's goalie camp the summer before.

"Watch his hips. Hips don't lie. Stay on the balls of your feet," Max chanted to himself as Bonner and the Algonquin offense twisted and passed into his territory. Bonner dodged the Powhatan defense, one man at a time. He torqued around them like a Texas tornado, leaving them scrambling on slides, three feet behind him.

Max kept his eyes on Bonner's hips. He saw him fake a pass to the left across the goal, and move to go behind the crease. His head turned, but his hips still faced the front of the crease. Max swerved to block Bonner's angle. He watched Bonner smoothly cradle the ball, moving it back and forth, back and forth, keeping his stick light and loose as a wand in his hands. Then, just as Max was almost mesmerized by the motion, Bonner froze, pivoting

Question Mark

on one foot. As Bonner suddenly changed the direction of his momentum, Max took his eyes off his opponent's hips and glanced at his stick. For a split second, the stick stopped, and Max saw the legendary eyes on the head—the yellow bloodshot orbs that proclaimed Johnny Bonner as Snake Eyes.

Max shuddered, and looked at Johnny's face behind the grill of his helmet. Even his real eyes seemed yellow. Max heard him bark out, "Later, Loser!" as he switched hands and spun into what

Max recognized as a question mark shot, one of the hardest to defend. Bonner focused the snake eyes on his stick head at the bottom right of the goal and spat the ball out of the pocket. Max dove down, stick out, on his knees in the crease to save a shot that wasn't there. Bonner hadn't taken a shot; instead he had passed the ball, and a nameless Algonquin attackman gently dinked Bonner's lightning assist into the top left corner of the goal. The only question mark was in Max's mind.

The vacuum of sound left by the stunned Powhatans sucked up the wild cheering of Algonquin fans. A hand grabbed Max and lifted him from the heap he had become on the ground. He looked up and saw Johnny Bonner looming over him.

"That wasn't even my best move, Shrimp. If you can't tell a shot from a pass, you'd better look for a new position."

Chapter Two

At the top of the hill, Polly Speyer did a 360 on her skateboard, pushed off twice to gain momentum, and coasted toward home. Her backpack bulged with library books for research on her project for the fifth grade's Medieval Day, her softball glove, several granola bars, a bruised apple, and a big water bottle. It was too full to zip, but she figured the weight would help her make it all the way home without having to pump again.

Her strawberry blond hair flew out from her helmet like a comet's tail. As she rounded the last curve before her house, she heard a shout, felt a *whizzzz* right under her nose, and collided with her twin, Max. Polly flailed her arms trying to catch her balance, and they landed in a tangled heap in the

grass. Champ, their Jack Russell terrier, or Jack Russell terror as the family sometimes called him, jumped on them and began barking, while joyfully licking their faces as if he had just tackled them single handedly. Books and granola bars lay every-where, and the water bottle rolled down the hill until it came to a stop at the foot of their neighbor Dr. Bob's driveway

"Yard sale!" cried Max.

Polly untangled herself from the pile and asked, "Max, what are you doing? I almost made it home on just two pumps!" Three pumps from the top of the hill was the Speyer twins' record.

"I'm sorry Pol. I was just practicing with Kyle." Max pointed at their first grade neighbor who was standing near the goal in the front yard of their yellow shingled house. He was holding one of his FiddleSTX™, a tiny lacrosse stick, obviously eager to keep playing with Max.

Max lowered his voice, "His aim isn't so good yet, and I wanted to get the ball before it rolled down the hill." He tossed the ball he had just saved to Polly. "We've already lost six this afternoon. I couldn't go after the ones that got away because I promised his mom that if he practiced with me, I wouldn't leave him alone. This is our last ball."

"But didn't you just get home from a game?" Polly asked as she started to pick up her books and granola bars. "Why are you out here already?"

"I need all the practice I can get," said Max gloomily.

Before Polly could ask about the game, they heard Mrs. Hannan, Kyle's mother, calling from his house. They walked him up the hill, and Max said, "Thanks for the workout, man. Keep practicing those high-to-lows and you're going to have a mean shot one day." Kyle strutted into his house with his chest puffed out and his head high.

"Goodbye, guys!" he called from the door. "I'm going to get my mom to bring me to one of your games, Max!"

"The last thing I need is a fan club," Max mumbled to Polly as they turned to walk away.

"I don't think you have to worry," she laughed, punching him lightly in the arm. "Let's just go get those balls and my water bottle before it gets run over." They walked down the hill, and found the balls in a heap of newspapers at the foot of Dr. Bob's driveway. The twins had lived up the street from Dr. Bob since they were two. He had an Australian shepherd named Carl who was Champ's best friend. They often took the dogs to the dog park to play together when Dr. Bob was in town. He was a sports psychologist, and, although the twins weren't exactly sure what that meant, he was always interested in hearing about their games.

"Dr. Bob must be on another trip," said Max.

"He goes to some pretty cool places to watch sports. I wonder where he is now?"

"He could be anywhere," said Polly. "Last time I saw him, he had just come home from playing golf in Scotland, and he was getting ready to go help some people practice for the Olympics. I haven't seen him in a while. I'll put his papers on the porch for him. You get the balls."

When they got back to their yard, Champ was tussling with one of Max's big goalie gloves.

"Aw, cut it out Champ," grunted Max. He grabbed Champ and wrestled his glove out of the little dog's determined jaws. He tossed it on the step. Champ, ready for an afternoon snack, bounded after it and dragged it through the doggie door to his lair in the basement.

"Champ's going to have a feast on that," said Polly. "Remember what he did to my shin guards?"

"Who cares?" said Max, plopping down in the grass to lie back and stare at the sky.

"Who cares?" asked Polly, "The Powhatan's youngest ever starting goalie cares. Or at least you should care. Mom would have a cow if she thought you were playing lacrosse without every pad ever invented."

"Mom won't be so worried about me when I'm warming the bench," he said. "I've never heard of anybody getting injured there. I see the headlines

now: 'Goalie, hospitalized after falling off bench into water bottles.'"

Polly knelt in front of Max, and pulled him to a sitting position. Even though they were twins, Max was small for his age, and she was a strong girl who played several sports herself. "What's the matter with you today?" she asked. "You've got the quickest hands in the fifth grade. I can never score on you. That's why Coach Rollman chose you to play on the select team. It's why you begged Mom to buy you that Xtreme stick." She picked up his remaining glove and rubbed it in his mop of dark red hair, "And these gloves, too, I might add."

"What a waste," Max groaned, and he shut his hazel eyes so he wouldn't have to think about it.

Max practiced harder than anyone Polly knew. He was always begging her to come out in the front yard and shoot on him. *Inside Lacrosse* magazine was his bible, and he spent as many hours as his mother would allow glued to ESPN-U studying college goalie techniques. Polly knew something big was up when Max didn't even react to the glove messing up his hair.

"Mom's going to be furious if you just let Champ eat that, Max. 'Waste not, want not,' remember?"

"How could I forget?" Max asked. Mrs. Speyer was a kindergarten teacher at Max and

Polly's school, Thomas Nelson Elementary. She had a catchy rule for every situation, and she firmly expected her twins to practice what she preached.

"Go get your glove from that crazy dog and let's board until dinner," Polly said.

Max and Polly had built a series of jumps on their front steps last summer, and until Max had gone to goalie camp, they spent hours on them every day. But at camp, Max had gotten lax fever pretty bad, and he hadn't been doing much skateboarding since. When he couldn't convince Polly to shoot on him, he would stand in the front yard in a crease he had painted around his goal and talk himself through his goalie moves: 'Get big, step out, back left, punch, jam, widen!' Polly understood his dedication to training, but sometimes when he started to shout these commands to invisible defensemen, she saw the neighbors shake their heads and laugh.

When Max came out of the basement with a half gnawed glove, Polly grabbed her board and ran to the front of the walk. "Air 180, backside landing, 360 finish," she shouted as she sped toward the jump. She leapt into the air with a spin, landed backwards, and spun completely around.

She looked triumphantly at Max, whom she expected to be ready to top her performance. He just sat on the porch steps playing with the yellow daffodils in one of Mrs. Speyer's many red clay pots.

"Max, what happened today?" She asked, sitting next to him. Max and Polly loved sports more than anything. There were some they were better at than others, but Max was never this down. "You weren't even this bummed when you broke your arm and couldn't play on the rec soccer team last year."

"I started in goal today, like I hoped. Some older guys, like Pat and Dan, were even telling me they were glad I was on the team, and how much they wanted to beat the Algonquins this year. And I was playing great—until overtime."

"Then what?" asked Polly.

"Then Snake Eyes got to me."

Polly scrunched up her freckled face in confusion, and Max reminded her, "Snake Eyes. You know, Johnny Bonner."

"The guy from Keswick?"

"Yeah. He has the fastest shot in the league—88 miles an hour—and he thinks he can fake out any goalie. They call him 'Snake Eyes,' and he even has these mean yellow eyes painted on his stickhead," said Max to the daffodils, knowing how pathetic he sounded.

"Well, how did you get to overtime if he's so great?" asked Polly.

"I did what Coach told me—kept my eyes on his hips."

"So how'd he get that last goal?" asked Polly, who knew that hips don't lie.

"I don't know, Pol. I looked at his eyes and thought he was shooting. He set me up and dropped a dime."

"Which eyes?" asked Polly.

"The snake eyes on his stick," groaned Max.

Polly rolled her eyes. "You need to get that guy out of your head, Max. He's just painted those eyes on his stick to freak people out. What did Coach Rollman do?" she asked. She knew he was a tough coach, especially with the select team. He had been a starting player for the University of Virginia Cavaliers when they won their first national championship, and Max and Polly's dad had gone to business school with him. Mr. Speyer was always reminding the twins that Coach Rollman had held Atlantic Coast Conference shooting records and saying that he was a great guy for coaching the Powhatans.

"He seemed more disappointed with the defense. I think he thought it was their problem, but he never blames any one person. He always says, 'Win as a team, lose as a team.' But I knew. It was Snake Eyes."

"Forget about that guy," said Polly. "Here, Board King," she reached over and grabbed Max's skateboard off the grass, "let's see your specialty—high looping double 360."

"You're right." Max stood up and shook himself all over. He stepped on his board and gave two powerful pushes. He flew over the jump, did a perfect 360 in the air, landed, sped around the curve, hit a crack in the sidewalk, and bailed out onto the grass.

"Board King, Ahnnnnnh!" He made the sound of a buzzer. "Loser!"

Chapter Three

Since they were a select team, the Powhatans had two games and two practices each week. After the Algonquin game, Max didn't mention how things were going, but he was out in the yard practicing with Polly every free minute he had. When she was busy with softball practice or her Medieval Day project, he got Kyle to come do his puff shots on him.

Polly had noticed doodles of reptilian eyes all over Max's math notebook, and she was a little worried. Max worked really hard at lacrosse, which was one of the reasons she thought he'd been chosen for this team in the first place. But she didn't want him to obsess about it anymore. He hadn't done any work on his project for Medieval Day, a special fifth grade day that the twins had looked

forward to since kindergarten. In fact, she wasn't even sure if he had an idea yet. She knew their mom was expecting both of them to come up with something creative. She tried to get him to think about something else—homework, skateboarding, or even Mr. Sachar, their crazy history teacher—but when she talked about school, all he'd say was, "Don't remind me. I've got enough to worry about."

Since the twins were big enough to sit in booster seats, Friday night had always meant pizza at The Upper Crust for the Speyers. Robert, the manager, was a great guy who always had a table saved for them and kept their lemonades filled to the brim.

He now brought an enormous steaming pizza to the table and set it on the spiral stand. "Double pepperoni, double cheese and jalapeno peppers. Where do you kids put all this pizza?" he laughed. "Must be all those sports you play. What are you up to now?"

"Softball," answered Polly.

Max loaded a molten slice onto his plate and hoped Robert would head to the next table. But this was Virginia, in the springtime, and the Cavaliers had a hot lacrosse team. Their senior attackman was touted to be a forerunner for the Tewaaraton trophy that went to the best player in the nation, and nobody was going to miss an opportunity to talk about the fastest sport on two feet.

"What about you, Maximus?" asked Robert. "You're bound to be playing lacrosse. Didn't you play goalie last year?"

Max nodded and motioned that his mouth was filled with burning cheese. Never one to miss an opportunity to promote one of his children, Mr. Speyer said, "Max is the starting goalie for the Powhatans this year. First fifth grader ever to start in goal for the under-13 team, right Max?"

Max kept chewing and nodded.

"We're finally going to beat those Algonquins this year with you in the goal, son," continued

Max's dad. "Max went to Pilat's last summer and he's really getting his technique down. They're 3-and-1 already, and they're taking the Algonquins down when they meet again at the end of the season." He looked hard at Max like he wanted him to say something.

Max kept looking down and poked two holes in his pizza, wishing his dad would change the subject. But Mr. Speyer had locked in and was starting to recite stats.

"Max had twelve saves in the first game, right Max?"

"Uh, right, Dad," Max said, wondering if he'd ever have twelve saves again in his life.

Polly looked at the pizza on Max's plate and thought, *Snake Eyes*. She was about to interrupt and distract her dad when the next table called for their check.

Robert said, "Bagataway, man. Have a great season," and went to take care of the other customers.

All through dinner, Polly tried to get her dad off the subject of lacrosse. She tried bringing up her softball team. Since her father was one of the coaches, mentioning the team would normally ensure his undivided attention, but tonight the conversation kept returning to lacrosse. She knew Max was doomed when Mr. Speyer picked up a long loaf of Italian bread. He stood up, and holding it in front of himself, started demonstrating how Max should punch his hands out first when he stepped into a save.

"You know, Max, Coach Rollman is a great athlete. You really want to work hard for him. If you keep this up, you might even be able to play college lacrosse someday. You could even play Division I. I think I'll call him and talk about the possibilities." He pulled out his Blackberry™ and started to write a memo to himself.

Mrs. Speyer put her hand gently on her husband's arm. "Not at dinner, Sweetie. This is family time."

Mr. Speyer shrugged and put the Blackberry™ back in his pocket. "Just hug the pipe and get there first," he said, waving his hand in front of him to emphasize his advice. "And remember, you're a winner." He poked his index finger dramatically at Max.

"Sure, Dad," said Max, gently backing away from the finger. "I'll try to remember that."

"Well," said Mrs. Speyer, "You've got a big game tomorrow. Early to bed, early to rise. We'd better finish dinner and get home."

Max and Polly looked at each other across the sea of crumpled napkins and pizza crusts. She winked at him, but he didn't wink back.

As they walked out to their car, a Jeep Cherokee pulled into the parking lot. It was filled with college students and covered with stickers that read UVA Lax, CASCADE, LAXWORLD, and Go 'Hoos. Mr. Speyer started to say something, but Polly cut him off.

"Did I tell you what I'm doing for Medieval Day this year?" she asked brightly, knowing her mom would want all the details.

Chapter Four

Saturday morning dawned a perfect Virginia spring day. The sky was blue with pink-tinted wisps of cirrus clouds, and the air was as cool as the steam off a popsicle. Forsythia, pear, and redbud branches were poised to burst into a ticker tape parade of watercolor blossoms. But it looked gray as November rain to Max as he packed up his gear for the game. In his head, he kept telling himself, *"Hug the pipe, left hand out, watch the shooter's stick,"* all the things his coaches had told him since he began playing in kindergarten. *"I've practiced this a million times. I know how to do this. I'm a winner,"* he kept saying. Finally he said it so forcefully, he heard it out loud, "I'm a winner!"

In the back of his head, however, he kept replaying the same bad movie—Johnny Bonner pulling back for a strike, looking at Max with yellow cobra eyes as the ball whizzed past into the net—upper right, lower right, upper left, lower left, and the five hole between his legs. And Max saw himself every time, just standing there mesmerized: *'Loser, loser, loser.'*

"Head case!" he said to himself. "Stop it!"

A good crowd of parents were out for the game against the Seminoles, and little brothers and sisters of the players ran everywhere, fooling with FiddleSTX™ and tossing Frisbees™ or just chasing each other. Everyone seemed happy and confident. Parents Max passed called encouragingly to him, "Hold that Pipe!" "Be the Wall!" or "Go Speyer!" He nodded politely and pretended he was focusing on the game.

During warm ups, Max and Cheese Dog, the Powhatans' back up goalie, took turns shooting on each other while the short sticks and poles did line drills. Cheese Dog, known to grownups as Charles Doggett, was a year older and twenty-five pounds heavier than Max. Although Max had been thrilled when Coach told him he'd be starting ahead of Cheese Dog, he now wondered if it was really such a good idea. When they finished their drills, Reeves, Chris, and the rest of the attack came down to shoot on the goalies. Balls flew everywhere, more than half of them ending up in the net. *"I should have saved those shots,"* Max thought to himself. *"I can't believe I missed so many."*

Coach Rollman gathered the team for some last game plan reminders, but Max, too busy worrying about what would happen when he got in the game, didn't hear a word. He went through the motions of the cheer with no enthusiasm, and headed out to face the firing squad.

The referee blew the whistle for the face-off, starting a scramble in the center of the field. For the first time in his life, Max found himself praying that the ball would stay at the other end so he wouldn't have to touch it.

The Powhatan attack was revved up. They dominated until halftime, when they were up by two. Max had caught one wimpy shot on his right that wouldn't have gone in anyway, and his luck held when two close shots hit and bounced off the pipe.

Every time the ball came near the crease and didn't go in, he could hear the fans cheering him on, shouting "Way to go, Speyer! Take it to the Max."

Trying to sound like a confident goalie, he called out to Tim, whom everyone called the Hammer, "Jam, jam, Tim! Check, shot," and to Pat, the silent long stick warrior, "Get in the hole!" but he wondered why they should even listen to him.

By the time the whistle blew for halftime, he was exhausted from worrying about trying to do the things that had once come so easily and given him such a rush.

The second half dragged on forever. By the end of the third quarter, every muscle in Max's body ached from being on high alert. His throat was sore from forcing himself to keep up his banter. The Powhatan offense continued to dominate, with Chris chalking up more goals with his flashy stick

work, and Doug—a guy the others called Toes—flicking in a low shot from the edge of the crease. Max didn't even bother to keep track.

The Seminoles finally got a fast break, and Max went through every step of the save in his head as the red Seminole midfielder barreled towards him, *"Stick out, get big, watch his stick, which quarter is he shooting for?"*

The boy pulled back, shot, and the ball zinged right through Max's legs, the number five hole. They had been open as wide as the sky. The referee's arms shot up, the home crowd was noticeably silent, and Coach motioned for Max to come out.

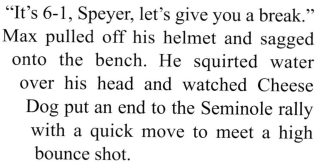

"It's 6-1, Speyer, let's give you a break." Max pulled off his helmet and sagged onto the bench. He squirted water over his head and watched Cheese Dog put an end to the Seminole rally with a quick move to meet a high bounce shot.

When the horn blew, ending the game a few minutes later, Polly came to the bench. She called out to his teammates, "Hey Toes, nice pick up on the crease. Good defense, Hammer." They raised their hands in acknowledgement, smiled, and thanked her. Max wondered how she knew those guys so well. He'd been on their team all season and didn't even feel comfortable with them.

"Good game, Goalie," she said when she got to Max.

"Give me a break, Pol. I felt like I was in quicksand. I knew what to do, but by the time I could move, the play was over. Without our attack, I'd be..." He drifted off, thinking about what a short reign he'd had as starting goalie.

"I don't know what else to do. It's not like I don't practice all the time," he said, shoving his bulky pads into his bag. "I'm not slow—I can even beat some of our attack guys when we do wind sprints. I'm doing everything Coach tells me to do, but nothing's working anymore." He fought with the zipper on the bag for a minute, then stopped suddenly and looked down. "It's like those snake eyes put a curse on me."

"You need help, Max," said Polly. "I think you should talk to Dr. Bob when we get home."

Max looked up at her and nodded, suddenly hopeful. "That's a great idea. Why didn't I think of it? Do you think he's back yet?"

"We can take Champ and go see when we get home," said Polly. "I know he'll listen to you. Dr. Bob always listens to what we tell him."

"Yeah, and he might have a drill I could work on to get it together before I lose my spot on the team." Just then, Max felt a strong hand slam down on his back. He looked up to see his father.

"Great game, Son," he said, "You guys looked good out there, and you really whipped those Seminoles. It's too bad about that last goal. What you need to do is just keep your legs together and get big…" As they walked to the car, Mr. Speyer kept coaching Max, who just nodded and thought about how he could explain his problem to Dr. Bob when he saw him.

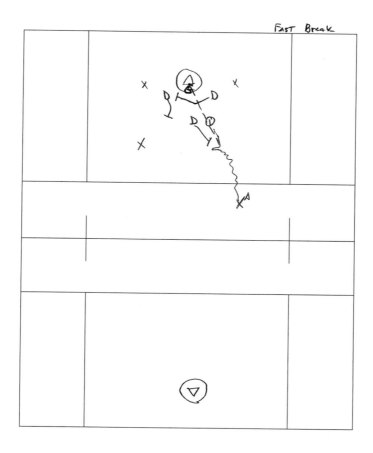

Chapter Five

An hour later, Max and Polly headed down the street with Champ dancing at the end of his orange and blue leash. He chased the few butterflies that flitted by, not seeming to care that Max's whole lacrosse career was on the line. Making a mad leap at a Monarch, he nearly jerked Polly's arm from her socket. She picked him up and carried him until they got to Dr. Bob's red front door. She sat him down, told him to stay, and unclipped his leash. She looked at Max and said, "I hope he's here," before ringing the bell.

Dr. Bob answered the door with his glasses shoved into his rumpled hair and a short green golf pencil tucked over his ear. Behind his glasses, his dark eyes crinkled as he smiled broadly at the twins.

"Max! Polly! How are you?" Dr. Bob was probably as old as their grandfather, but he was so energetic it was impossible to tell. Even though he traveled all around the world going to golf tournaments and other sporting events to work with athletes, he never seemed too tired to visit with them. Max was just glad he was home today.

"Champ, did you bring your people for a walk?" Dr. Bob asked, bending down to scratch the little terrier behind his collar.

Champ wiggled in pleasure, then barked and took off into the house, not shy about his welcome. They heard Carl lumber from under Dr. Bob's desk, and suddenly the hall was full of wagging tails and panting tongues.

"Sit," said Dr. Bob, as he took a webbed leash from the hall tree. The two dogs lowered themselves closer to the floor, quivering with anticipation. "Mmm-hmm." He cleared his throat gruffly, and the dogs dropped a little further. He looked at them seriously, raising his eyebrows. Finally, their tail ends touched the ground long enough for Polly and Dr. Bob to clip on their leashes before they leapt up and headed out the door. Carl and Champ were a funny team. Little Champ yapped and growled, spinning around patient Carl like a Tasmanian devil. Carl kept gently pushing Champ with his muzzle, herding him back to the group.

As they headed up the hill past Kyle's house toward the dog park, Dr. Bob stretched one arm over his head and took a deep breath. "What a fine day," he said, "I'm glad you came and rescued me from my computer."

"Have you been on a trip, Dr. Bob?" asked Polly.

"Yes," said Dr. Bob. "The Masters is coming up in about a month, and one of the golfers I work with wanted some help with his putting. I went to Florida to watch him play in a tournament."

"Wow," said Max. "Did you go to Disney World? Lots of lacrosse teams go there for Spring Break."

"I didn't get to Disney World this time. I was in Miami. Florida's got some great golf courses," said Dr. Bob. "But what have you been up to?" he asked, looking from Max to Polly. "If I know you two, you've already played three rounds of something today."

Max had never asked Dr. Bob for any advice about his sports; he figured he got enough of that from his coaches and his dad. Polly was the only person he'd ever admitted his problems to. But as they walked through the neighborhood, up the hill toward the dog park next to the library, he started explaining what had been going on. Once he began, he found that he couldn't blurt it out fast enough.

He told Dr. Bob about making the team, how happy he had been, and how hard he had practiced.

He told him about the game against the Algonquins, and how he couldn't get Johnny Bonner's eyes out of his head. "I know this sounds stupid, Dr. Bob," he finished, "But when he called me a loser, it's like he put a curse on me. Nothing works anymore. I know you know a lot about golf, but do you know anything about lacrosse that could help me?"

Dr. Bob chuckled and said, "I'm sure it does feel like a curse, Max, but I'm also sure there's something more logical going on. I actually used to be a college lacrosse coach, but to tell you the truth, it doesn't sound like there's much of a problem with your lacrosse. Let me think for a minute."

They walked on, the silence only broken by Champ's gleeful barks. When they reached the dog park, they stopped and looked out at the velvet Blue Ridge Mountains to the west before they opened the iron gate and went in. It was unusually quiet for a Saturday afternoon. Only one other person was there, a man reading a newspaper while two big yellow labs and a little black and white spaniel played. Max knew the dogs—their names were Woody, Otto, and Boots—but he could never remember the man's name, even though Dr. Bob had introduced them before. Polly waved at him, and he waved back at the group before going back to his reading.

"Too much train," said Dr. Bob finally. "And not enough trust." He sat down on a wooden bench

and took Carl off his leash. Polly unhooked Champ and the twins sat down with Dr. Bob as the dogs ran off to sniff everything in sight.

"What do you mean?" asked Max.

"What I mean is this," said Dr. Bob. "You know you're a good athlete. Your coach is smart, he's chosen you for the team, and he's playing you ahead of a bigger, older goalie. You pay close attention to what your coach tells you and you practice all the time. But now, I believe it's time for you to stop practicing and start playing. When you go into a game, you've got to quit training and start trusting the work you've done to get there. It's important to trust that you have the skills you need to play the part your coach has chosen you to play. Training and trusting—they go hand-in-hand, and they've got to stay balanced."

"But what about Snake Eyes?" asked Max.

"Every athlete has important rivals, and it's good to respect their skills. This boy has those snake eyes on his stick to intimidate you and make you think he's tough. And you'd better assume he's tough if you're going to get strong enough to beat him. If he's a snake, picture yourself as an eagle, swooping down on him. Visualize that several times a day—especially before you go to bed at night and right before your game. Then, when you've done everything you can do to get ready for the game, when you've practiced every one of your moves until you can do them in your sleep, stop thinking about mechanics. You have to go into your games relaxed and confident in yourself. Don't worry about your opponent, and don't try harder. Do what you know how to do, and you'll do your best."

Dr. Bob called to Champ and Carl who were romping around the man with the paper. When they returned, he took an old tennis ball out of the pocket of his red sweater and threw a high lob toward the thick oak trees at the far side of the park. Champ and Carl raced after it. As the ball neared the ground, both dogs hurled themselves toward it. Champ's little muzzle closed on it a split second before Carl got there, and with Carl at his side, he brought it proudly back to Dr. Bob.

"Train and trust," said Dr. Bob, as he rubbed the panting dogs' heads. "These guys don't worry about who caught the ball last time or if they can do it again. They just love doing it."

"Train and trust," said Max. "It makes sense, but how do I do it?"

"Give yourself a mental cue, a sign that will remind you to stop worrying about the game and just play. Use your cue regularly, and it will help your performance. Reminding yourself to relax will let all that training kick in, and free it up for you to use it."

"What kind of cue?" asked Max.

Dr. Bob looked at Max and smiled. "Anything you want can be your cue, Max, as long as you remember to do it every time. Double knot your cleats, clap three times, any action that reminds you to relax and trust your body to do what you've trained it to do."

"Train and trust," said Max again, thinking out loud. "I'll try it. Thanks, Dr. Bob."

"You're welcome, Max. And also, remember you're on a team, and a good one from the sound of it. You don't have to do this all by yourself. Trust your teammates, too." He threw the ball, now covered in slobber, high into the air again. The dogs shot after it.

They took turns throwing the ball to the dogs. Sometimes Carl would retrieve it, sometimes Champ. Before they all headed home, they stopped at the water fountain, just the right height for dogs. As Champ and Carl slurped up the water, Dr. Bob smiled at the twins. "Thanks again for getting me and Carl out this afternoon. And keep me posted on how your season goes."

Max said, "Thanks for the advice, Dr. Bob." Although he had no idea how it would actually help him, he decided he trusted Dr. Bob enough to give it a try.

Chapter Six

Max kept practicing as hard as ever, but he also took Dr. Bob's advice. Every night before he fell asleep, he pictured himself soaring out of the goal into the deep blue sky and barreling back down, talons extended, snatching up the snake that was trying to slither into his crease. At practice and in games when he found himself obsessing about his technique, he'd take his stick and tap it on his face mask three times until his head cleared and he regained that blue sky feeling.

As the spring evenings quickly lengthened and the season went on, the Powhatans continued to win games. Max still had Polly out shooting on him until dark every day after practice. Polly noticed that there were still snake eyes in the margins of Max's notebooks at school, but now she also saw talons surrounding them. She kept trying to get him do a little more homework, but every time she suggested that they work on their Medieval Day projects together, he grumpily assured her he had it under control.

One afternoon after practice, Max couldn't find Polly. He supposed she was up at the library working on her project. It struck him that perhaps he should do some work on his, but he quickly pushed that thought out of his mind, saying, *"I've got a game tomorrow. I need to practice."* He threw his duffel with all his goalie gear and his backpack on the porch, yelled to his mother through the open window that he was home, and went to find Kyle.

When he got there, Kyle was bugging his mother to let him watch *The Incredibles* while she was trying to make dinner. "What a marvelous idea!" she said when Max asked if Kyle could come shoot on him. The two boys headed down the street, and Max was surprised to see Polly out front, setting up the skateboard jump. Dan was helping her carry it, and Hammer and Cheese Dog lounged on the front steps. All of Max's gear was in the grass.

"Hey, Max, come ride with us," Polly called. "I'm going to show these guys my 180, and Dan's going to teach me some new jumps. You can show them your specialty." Obviously Polly didn't remember he had wiped out the last time he had tried it.

"Uh, Kyle and I need to practice," he said lamely.

Hammer called out to him from the steps, "Aw, man, you don't need to practice. Coach told us to take it easy before the game and get some rest." He patted the step next to him. "Here, guy, have a seat and watch the show."

Kyle looked at Hammer's big biceps as if he were Mr. Incredible, and then he looked back at Max. "Can we sit with him, Max?" he asked.

"There goes the fan club," thought Max, but he laughed, and said "Sure. Let's see what they can do." They sat and watched Polly and Dan fly over the jump, sometimes landing upright, sometimes wiping out in the grass. Hammer and Cheese Dog ribbed them, booing and cheering, and generally making so much noise that Mrs. Speyer came out on the porch to see what was going on.

She smiled when she saw the boys from the team. After she greeted them, she told Max and Polly, "Have fun. It'll be dinner time in about forty-five minutes."

Max was surprised she didn't tell them to come in and do homework. She usually insisted that he and Polly get started before dinner. Cheese Dog called out, "Showtime," and started the banter up again.

Forgetting about the last time he had ridden his skateboard, Max hopped up and shouted to Polly, "Pass me my stick, Sister. One high looping

360 coming up." Polly pushed the skateboard down the sidewalk to him. He took two pumps up the driveway, pivoted, and charged back down toward the jump. He flew over the top and twisted through the motions. He felt so light. He wanted to stay in the air forever, with everyone whooping and laughing around him, and the board pressed tight against his feet, following his every move. When he finally landed, he did an extra 360 at the end, hopped off, and called out, "Board King!" Everybody laughed and cheered.

Kyle looked at him like he was a rock star for just a flash, before he returned to watching Hammer, and Dan grabbed the board for the next jump. It was dark when Mrs. Speyer came back outside and said, "I hate to break this party up, but your dinner's on the table."

"What?" asked Max, surprised. "We just got started."

"Why don't you walk Kyle on home, and then come wash up quickly," said his mom.

"Sorry we didn't practice, Max," said Kyle. "I know you have a game tomorrow."

"Don't worry, Kyle," said Max. "I think I'll be ready."

As the season wound to an end, the Powhatans were 10-and-3. Proud of the team, Coach Rollman was starting to talk about a trip to summer festivals in Baltimore and New York to give them the competition that would take them to the next level. Max did all the things that Dr. Bob had told him to do, but he wasn't sure if it was the visualizing or all the extra practice time he put in that kept him from freezing in the goal the way he had in front of Snake Eyes. Except for the one evening he had

skateboarded with Polly and the guys from the team, he still spent time before every game practicing and worrying about how good the other team might prove to be.

But, as Dr. Bob had supposed, the Powhatans were strong. Even though Max feared he wasn't helping them much, his starting spot was never jeopardized, and Cheese Dog got plenty of time in goal. Everybody was feeling revved up to beat the Algonquins in the final game of the season. But every time Max thought about the Algonquins, panic squeezed his heart like a boa constrictor.

The night before the big game, the Speyers sat in The Upper Crust, waiting for their pizza. Mrs. Speyer had asked Max if he wanted to invite Charles or Dan or some of the guys from the team to join them. "No thanks, Mom," Max said. "Those guys are great, but I just want to chill. And his name is Cheese Dog."

Even though it would have been fun to hang out with the older boys some more, Max had decided that family pizza on Friday seemed to be working for his game. Maybe his mom was right about the carbo loading. And, even if his dad was still pouring on the coaching tips, it seemed better to stick to the routine.

"So, son, are you ready for tomorrow? You know, I could take you out tonight and shoot on you, give you some pointers. You need to…"

Polly interrupted him, and said, "Dad, could you please pass the bread?" before her dad could try to use it as a teaching tool.

"Thanks, Dad," said Max, "but I'm as ready as I'll ever be. I've practiced all spring, and now I've just got to do what I know how to do. Train and trust, right?"

"Mmm," said his dad, "Train and trust, that's all right. But when you're *mano a mano* with that Bonner kid, you can't forget to…"

"This is by far the best pizza in town," said Mrs. Speyer. "You'd better eat some more, Max, so you'll have energy for tomorrow."

"Carbo loading," said Max.

His mom beamed, happy to see he had been listening to her. "That's right! And have some more salad, too. You can't beat the anti-oxidants in those leafy greens."

"I mean, I hear he has the best shot in the state," continued Mr. Speyer, waving a slice of pizza in the air to emphasize his point. Max ducked, afraid hot cheese would fly off in his direction.

"I think it's the best pizza in the world," said Polly, winking at Max. "Eat up!"

Chapter Seven

The next morning, about forty-five minutes before the game, Max lugged his big black duffel to the bench. Max was early, and with its fresh chalk lines, the field looked like the Jolly Green Giant in war paint. Soon, a few Powhatans and Algonquins trickled in. He heard someone call out, "Go Bonner!" and he knew Snake Eyes had arrived.

Calmly, Max put on his pads one by one and tightened his cleats. As he put on his gear, he pictured himself making saves, like an eagle swooping down on the ball. When he was suited up, he called to Cheese Dog, "Let's go loosen up before everybody gets here."

They took turns shooting on each other. Cheese Dog talked excitedly about taking the

Algonquins down. Max wanted to ask him to pipe down, but he really liked Cheese Dog, and he recognized that his enthusiasm, even from the bench, had been a big part of the Powhatans' winning season. As he went through his moves, Max just smiled and said, "That's right, man."

He watched Cheese Dog when it was his turn in goal. Cheese Dog was a good goalie, but every save he made seemed dramatic, a desperate gasp to hold on, rather than an efficient move. Suddenly, it came to Max that he could actually see the ball sooner and move to it more quickly than Cheese Dog could. That's why Coach was starting him over the older boy. And he realized that Cheese Dog, with more experience, could see that too. Max felt a surge of respect for the way Cheese Dog had treated him throughout the season. It would have been so easy for him to resent Max, but he just seemed to love being part of the team. How had he not noticed all this before?

After the warmups, Coach Rollman called the team over for the pre-game pep talk. "I don't have to tell you this is a big game, but I also don't have to tell you that you're a big team. Your record this season speaks for itself. Be present, keep your calm focus, and remember that there's nothing to save it for. Powhatans on three!" He put his fist down, called, "One, two, three, Powhatans!"

When they all roared "Powhatans!" Max felt the hair on his forearms rise up in goosebumps. He couldn't believe how excited he felt in anticipation of the game. He wasn't scared anymore—in fact, he felt like he was ready to do battle. Suddenly, he thought about the medieval knights they had been studying in school going out to defend their honor. He was going out to defend his honor against Snake Eyes. His pads were his armor, and his stick was his shield. Just as Max pulled his helmet over his face, it came to him in a flash—he finally knew what his Medieval Day project would be. He couldn't wait to tell Polly.

Cheese Dog slugged him on the shoulder and said, "Stay big, guy," and Max loped out to defend his castle. He had all the Powhatans with him, and together, they made quite a team.

"Come and get me Snake Eyes," he thought. *"I'm going to eat you up."*

The whistle blew and, after a lengthy struggle, the ball popped out of the face-off into an Algonquin midfielder's stick. He winged it across the field to an attackman, who spun back and passed it to another Algonquin behind the goal.

Max told himself he was an eagle, and all his senses felt heightened. He saw the ball wherever it flew and he was in position, ready to grab it. He watched the ball come out from behind the goal, and he called to Pat, his long stick middie, "Drop in the hole." He quickly surveyed his defense, "Dan, you're hot. Hammer, punch him out, widen, get some space."

Everybody shifted as he called out to them. He realized that at the beginning of the season he had been amazed when they followed his commands, but now he didn't even get a charge from these older boys doing what he told them to do. He had gotten to know these guys—thanks to Polly, he had to admit—and they trusted each other. This was a dance they had done many times. Everyone was in perfect step.

Johnny Bonner cut in front of him, ready to get the feed. Max called, "Check stick," to Pat. Pat couldn't get there in time, but Max followed Bonner with his body, mirroring his hips and watching only the ball. He cut off Bonner's angle and easily saved his high shot. He cleared it down-field, and the Powhatans dominated long enough for him to think, *"I beat Snake Eyes. Now I'm going to shut him out."*

The Algonquins picked up a loose ball and went back on the attack. The Powhatan defense shifted left as the Algonquins passed right. Pat stopped the fast break and Max settled his defense by calling out ball positions, "Top center, top left, back left," When the boy with the ball started to dodge around Dan, Max called, "Who's hot?"

"I've got to get in position," Max thought, "Got to shut them down."

Snake Eyes flashed in front of him as Algonquin number six dodged through the defenders in front of the crease. Six pulled back to shoot, then faked and fed it to Snake Eyes, who winged it right past Max.

As he felt the ball fly by him, his heart sank. He waited for the referee to shout, "Goal!" Then, amazingly, he felt the reverberation of the shot hitting the pipe. It bounced back into the crease. Algonquin and Powhatan sticks jabbed and tore at the ground in front of Max, but Dan pulled it out, carried it to midfield and lobbed it downfield to Reeves.

Max started talking to himself. He was babbling, "Left hand out, watch ball, shooters' stick, call out ball position, holds, checks...this is what I need to do to make saves." He wondered briefly about using his mental cue, but he decided he didn't have time.

The Algonquins started another slow break. Max watched his defense shift too far to the strong side where the ball was, but he was so busy coaching himself he didn't call out to them. Snake Eyes got the ball out on the wing and dodged by his man toward the goal. Max got as big as he could and, as Snake Eyes bore down on him, he looked at those evil eyes on the tip of the stickhead. He watched the eyes pull back for a top right shot. Snake Eyes threw a stick hitch, and Max threw his stick up to meet it. Snake Eyes finished high-to-low, tucking the ball softly into the left downstairs corner of the net.

The referee called the goal just as time expired in the first quarter. Pat and Dan tried to make Max feel better on the way to the bench, but he was too busy beating himself up to listen.

"Speyer," said Coach when they had gathered, "Shake it off. Everybody, you're playing their game. It's only 1-0 and you're letting them drag you around the field by the nose. Get out there and play your game. Forget about the technique, just watch the ball and play lacrosse. Remember what got you here."

Max looked out from the huddle at all the fans who had come to watch the game. He saw Polly with his Mom and Dad on the sidelines, and he saw Champ bouncing up and down in front of them. And, to his surprise, next to Champ he saw Carl and Dr. Bob. *"Wow,"* he thought. *"Dr. Bob came to my game."* He watched as Dr. Bob threw a lacrosse ball and Champ and Carl took off after it.

"It's time to trust," thought Max. *"Free it up."*

Max pulled his shoulders back and took a swig of water from the manager's six pack of bottles. He took his big goalie stick and touched it slowly to his head three times. "Trust," he said.

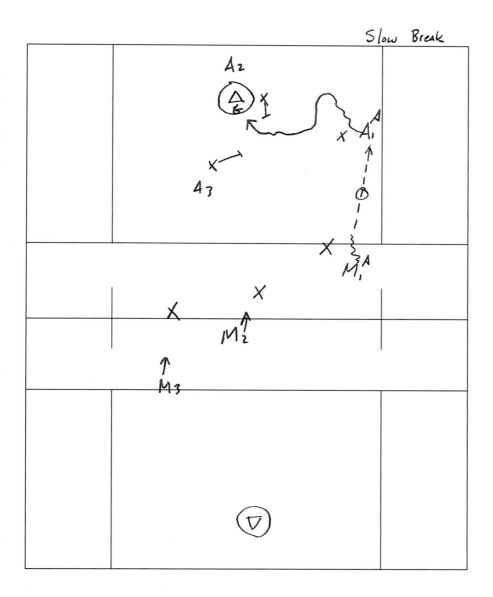

He didn't look at the Algonquins as he headed out to the goal. He looked up at the sky and down at the field, and he thought, *"This is Powhatan territory, and that's my crease."*

The whistle blew, and the ball popped out of the face-off into Powhatan control. As Max called out ball positions, he felt his mind hush, and the rhythm of the game took over. He was a warrior, and this was no game. This was all that mattered right now. The ball wasn't a piece of hard rubber, it was a skull, taken in battle by his tribe. Powerful

images of native Americans and knights, jousts and week-long lacrosse games, eagles and snakes swirled together in his head. He felt fierce.

Again, Snake Eyes headed toward him, cradling so fast the ball blurred. Max moved as if one with the ball. When he saw Snake Eyes lower his stick, Max instinctively got lower. When Snake Eyes pulled back, Max watched his hips, ready for the fake. Bonner twisted high and left, and shot. The ball went low and right, and Max flew to it. He saw the whites of Johnny Bonner's eyes widen in surprise behind the grid of his face mask. The spell was broken.

Again and again, the Algonquins shot on Max, but he was huge and they couldn't score. He filled the goal, and he seemed to be there before the attack had decided where to shoot. After halftime, the third quarter sped by. Cheese Dog had all the subs doing the wave, and their enthusiasm from the bench only increased the pulsing energy that flowed in Max's veins. But there was still no Powhatan score.

Coach Rollman pulled them in before the fourth quarter started. He said, "You're on fire, but you need to settle down and focus. They're ahead, and they have nothing to lose now by stalling. They're going to start playing keep away with you. Don't let them get to you. You've got to keep getting the ball and making plays until the last whistle blows."

Max never left the zone. When the Algonquins shot, he was there. When they pulled a play that the legendary Tom Marechek himself would have been proud of and scored on him, he shrugged it off and made the next save. The clock was ticking, but he didn't think about anything except where the ball was. He moved almost magnetically between it and the goal. He was an eagle, swooping down on his prey—a knight, defending his castle.

In front of him, the defense did their work. Pat, Dan and the other guys cleared the ball down the field. He watched excitedly as Chris did a beautiful question mark move and scored. The Powhatans were finally on the board, but they still trailed 2-1. The clock showed they had less than five minutes until the final horn blast. The Algonquin coach frantically signaled for a time out.

The Powhatans hustled in, excited about the goal. Coach Rollman's voice was calm and deep. "If we get possession, we settle the offense and get a good shot off. If they get the ball on the face-off, when the clock goes under four minutes, we go into Mad Dog. Wait to double their man with the ball until he gets behind the goal. Speyer, cover the crease. Got it? Powhatans on three." They roared out of the huddle.

Another face-off scrambled in the center of the field, this time with more urgency. Four and a half minutes remained on the clock. The Algonquins took control and worked the ball downfield, playing keep away, just as Coach Rollman had warned. Max glanced at the clock as it clicked under four minutes and called to his defense, "We're in Mad Dog!" Pat and Dan moved into position, double-teaming Snake Eyes. No matter which way he turned, one of the Powhatan defenders was there. At just the right moment when Snake Eyes rolled back to get free, Pat slammed a strong check on his stick. Snake Eyes was left in the dust as Dan picked up the loose ball and threw it back to Max, who lobbed it downfield to Chris. Chris ran in to the Powhatan goal, faked left, and scored, right through the number five hole. Max knew how the Powhatan goalie felt, but he didn't have long to think about it. They were tied at two, with less than two minutes remaining. If the Powhatans couldn't score, they'd be back in overtime with the Algonquins.

The face-off was a mess. It seemed as if every player on both teams was scrabbling to get the ball. Finally, Pat got control of the ball. Coach Rollman called "Settle" to the Powhatans, and the fans just yelled. Chris and Reeves exchanged passes, trying to get some control. Bobbing on his toes, twirling his stick in his fingers, Max watched his team set up and move in for the game-winning goal. Reeves ran around the Algonquin crease, but wherever he was, there was an Algonquin defender. He flicked the ball back to Chris. The clock was ticking down, and Max was ready to win this one. Finally, Chris got a window. He pulled back and shot, and the ball was headed in. The noise from the fans and the bench was deafening. The goalie lunged, and the ball sailed past him. Cheese Dog and the bench jumped up and down, high-fiving each other. The Powhatans on the field shook their sticks in the air and whooped.

But something was wrong. Instead of calling the goal, the referee waved his hands in front of himself, shouting, "No goal!"

"No goal?" Max couldn't believe it. He hadn't seen any fouls on the way down. It had been a clean shot. *"No goal?"* The referee sprinted to the crease and threw his hands towards the chalk circle. Boys on both teams muttered and milled around.

The referee turned to the box where the statisticians sat and boomed out, "Crease violation! No goal!"

He gave the ball to an Algonquin defender who sent it in a desperate Hail Mary toward Max.

As it flew across the midfield line, the horn went off, jarringly announcing that the Powhatans were back in overtime with the Algonquins. Max had been here before, and now it mattered more than ever. What was he going to do? He knew Snake Eyes was desperate to score on him. He shuddered just thinking about it. No wonder they called it sudden death.

Coach Rollman called the Powhatans to the bench, and the referee called the captains to the field to hear the overtime procedures. Max paid close attention as Coach explained the situation. "For you to win here, guys, you've got to get possession of the ground ball at the face-off. "He went over a special play called "Crash" that they had practiced for just such a situation. Crash depended on the midfielder on the wing getting the ball and creating the fast break. "Both your goals in this game have been on the fast break, Powhatans," he said seriously. "Always go with what brung you. Don't play to not lose here. You've got to go for the win."

Once the ball was in play, Max saw Pat move into position and execute the Crash play perfectly. He picked up the ground ball and lofted it to Hammer, who zinged it behind the goal to Chris. Chris spun and shot from the top of the box, but his shot ricocheted off the helmet of a defender desperately trying to move in its path. The ball hurtled back toward midfield. Chris tore after the loose ball, but Snake Eyes was there first. He stretched over the midfield line, snatched up the ball and headed downfield.

Max took a deep breath. Quickly, he touched his stick to his helmet, *one, two, three.* He shook himself loosely to relax, and got into position. Snake Eyes bore down on him. Algonquins called out, "Pass it Bonner! On your right!" but Snake Eyes kept coming. He spun past every last Powhatan between himself and Max, and then, they were alone on the field. Max didn't even bother looking at his eyes, but he could tell they were grimacing. Mirroring his hips, Max stayed with Bonner until he pulled back and bulleted the ball right to the hole at Max's left, the hardest spot for a right handed goalie to defend. Max twisted, throwing his hands out and his left elbow up. His stickhead clocked around, filling the hole, followed by his body, and Snake Eye's shot belonged to Max.

Snake Eyes stood planted, looking stunned, as Max winged the ball to Dan, who sent it in an un-broken chain of crisp Powhatan passes to Reeves. Reeves went in for the shot, but he saw Pat move to open space. He passed behind his back to Pat at the top of the box, and Pat stepped in and ripped it, long and low, into the goal, into sudden victory.

The final horn blew. The Algonquins, once such a powerhouse, faded into the sidelines. The

Powhatan bench streamed onto the field. They grabbed Pat and pulled him toward the crease, where they piled on Max. Coach Rollman hurried over, grinning like Max had never seen. Slapping his boys on the back, he seemed to have to visibly contain himself when he said, "Handshake, guys, and be cool." Max knew that Coach Rollman valued good sportsmanship, and he would never let his team over celebrate or rub a victory in their opponents' faces. But he could also tell how much this game had meant to his coach.

The Powhatans peeled themselves off the pile they had created in the crease and shook like dogs settling their fur after a bath. Putting on serious

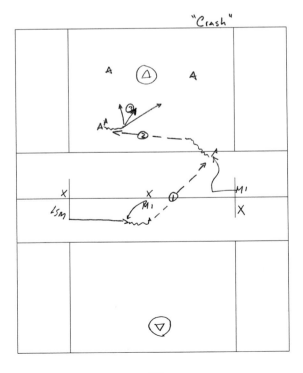

faces, they formed a long sweaty line. They held out their right hands and filed past the Algonquins. "Game," they said, each time they touched palms lightly, shorthand for "good game, nice work." "Game, game." Occasionally boys who knew each other well would punch each other in the arm and say something more specific. "Good D" or "Awesome shot." Max saw Snake Eyes, and he wondered what he should say.

When Max held out his hand, he just said "Game," like he did to everybody else. Just being able to treat Bonner like everybody else seemed amazing to Max. As he pulled his hand back, Bonner said, "Good game, Shrimp. You had it

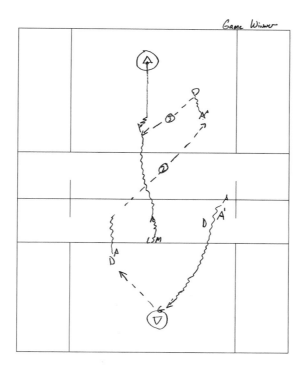

going on." Max looked up into the taller boy's eyes. He wanted to laugh when he saw that Bonner's fierce eyes were really light blue with long blond eyelashes. But no matter how sweet the Snake Eyes looked up close, Max had never been so proud to be called a shrimp in his life.

"Thanks, Johnny," he said.

After the handshaking, the Powhatans met back at the crease. Coach Rollman looked straight at Max and said, "You did it. You played lacrosse." He went on to point out individual highlights in what he described as a supreme team effort. He mentioned all the goals, and he congratulated the team on the way they handled the Crash play in overtime. Then he paused and said, "But, I think we all know who deserves the game ball." He held it out to Max. "I've always thought you had it, but today, it was like you finally trusted that you had it, too."

When Max walked over to the stands, his parents were talking with Dr. Bob and Polly. Everyone was buzzing about the game. "So exciting!" "What a finale!" "Wait till you take this show to Baltimore in the summer!" He held out the game ball to them and grinned.

"You played a great game, Max," said Dr. Bob. "You deserve that ball."

"Thank you," said Max. "I was such a head

case at the beginning of the season, but today I finally trusted that I could do it."

"Train and trust, that's what I always say," said Mr. Speyer. "But you also have to…"

"Mom," Max said quickly, "Did I tell you about the great idea I had for my Medieval Day project?"

Polly looked at him in surprise, knowing he had been really embarrassed when Mr. Sachar had asked for progress reports the day before.

"I'm building a shield, out of some of the extra wood we have from the jumps. I'm going to paint my symbol on it," said Max.

"That sounds like a wonderful idea, Max," said his mother, as they all started walking toward the cars. "What will your symbol be? They didn't have lacrosse in medieval times."

"No Mom, it's not lacrosse. It's an eagle," he said.

"Holding a snake!" laughed Polly, relieved that Max had finally come up with an idea. She and Dr. Bob smiled at each other.

"And what will your motto say on your shield, Max?" asked Dr. Bob.

Before Max could say "Train and trust," Kyle came bounding up, gripping his fiddlestick with Champ and Carl bouncing behind him.

"Max, you were awesome," he panted. "Do you think I can ever play as good as you?"

Max looked at Dr. Bob. His advice had worked so well. "Sure you will Kyle," he said, "If you keep trusting that great shot of yours."

Kyle grinned, his enthusiasm making up for his lack of teeth. "Will you keep throwing with me?"

Max took the little stick and tapped it on Kyle's head three times. He put the game ball in the pocket and handed it back to Kyle.

"Sure I will," said Max.

GLOSSARY

Lacrosse, often called "lax," has many wonderful expressions, about playing the game and its history. Lacrosse is known as the fastest sport on two feet, and it is also the fastest growing youth sport today. If you are interested in learning more about playing lacrosse or the history of the game, you can contact U.S. Lacrosse and the Lacrosse Museum and National Hall of Fame at 113 W. University Parkway, Baltimore, MD 21210, 410-235-6882, *www.uslacrosse.org*, or you can order *Inside Lacrosse* magazine or get information to download at Inside Lacrosse, 701 East Pratt Street, Suite 100, Baltimore, MD 21202, 888-367-2860, *www.insidelacrosse.com.*

Bagataway: Bagataway (bah-**gat**-a-way) is a Native American name for the game of lacrosse. Lacrosse was the first team sport in North America. North American tribes played games covering miles, with up to 1000 players on a side. These lacrosse games were religious and cultural components of tribal warfare and welfare.

Checking: Checking is a defensive method of using the stick to hit the offensive player's stick or gloves in order to knock the ball out of his stick pocket. Checking can distract and intimidate an offensive player who is trying to make an assist or shot.

Close Defender: The close defender is one of three defensive players that guard the opposing three attack players. These defenders position themselves "close" to the goal area they are defending with their goalie.

Crease: The crease is a circle with a nine-foot radius (nine feet from the center of the goal to the edge). It is drawn around the goal to protect the goalie and make it more challenging for the offense to score. Offensive players are not allowed to enter the crease. Defensive players can go into the crease if they don't have the ball, and they can receive a pass while standing inside the crease.

DI, DII, DIII: The National Collegiate Athletic Association (NCAA) places college varsity teams into divisions based on the size of the school and the number of scholarships awarded. The largest schools are Division I and the smallest are Division III. Only DI and DII schools offer athletic scholarships.

Dime: Dime is slang for an assist.

Dodger: The dodger is an offensive player with the ball who is in a threatening position to score.

Face-off: The face-off is the play that starts each quarter and restarts the game after a goal is scored. The ball is placed on the ground at the center of the field between two opposing players' stick heads. When the referee blows the whistle the two players move their sticks and bodies to gain possession of the ball or they maneuver the ball to one of their two wing men. The wing men are positioned twenty yards to the side of the face off, across from their teammate who is facing off. Wing men can only pick up the loose ball; they cannot collide with the other players in the face off.

Fast Break: When the ball goes quickly from the defensive end of the field to the offensive end, it is usually because the goalie makes a clearing pass to a breaking (running free) player. The goalie's offense then pushes to the goal for a shot before the other team's defense can get in position. This gives the fast breaking team a 4 versus 3 advantage and forces the defense to slide. The fast break usually gets a shot off after just one or two passes.

GLE: The GLE (goal line extended) is an imaginary line that goes across the field from sideline to sideline on the same plane as the goal. A dodger in front of the GLE is in a position to score. Defenders want to keep dodgers behind the GLE, where they are not in a position to score.

High-to-Low Shots: High-to-low shots (also called changing planes) are a way the shooter can trick the goalie. The shooter starts with the stick head held high and finishes the shot with the stick head toward the ground. The goalie is taught to move in the same plane (level) as the shooter's stick head. By changing planes, the shooter forces the goalie to commit to moving in to make a save. The goalie is tricked into moving to a place where the shot is not going. This is the most effective shot in lacrosse because of the deception and simplicity of the move. The shooter can even hide the stick behind his back and head. He then shoots in one motion straight over the top of his shoulders to the goal.

Jam, Punch, Widen: These words are commands that the goalie calls out to his teammates who are guarding the ball. The goalie tells the defender to move the man with the ball away from the goal so the defender can recover. It is legal for a defender to punch his hands at the front body of an offensive player, as long as the defender keeps both hands on his stick and only his gloves are touching the offensive player. But, if the defender reaches his stick in front of the dodger, the referee calls a cross check violation. Then, the defender must sit in the penalty box for one minute, and the offense has an extra player advantage until the penalty time expires.

Long Stick Middie: A long stick middie is a defensive specialist at the midfield. Teams are allowed a maximum of four long sticks on the field at once. With the three close defenders guarding the three attackmen, teams will replace a short stick middie with a long stick midfielder in order to get a greater defensive advantage. Long stick middies usually guard the top offensive midfielder on the opposing team. The longer stick can be more effective in checking and bothering the offensive player with the ball.

Mad Dog: Mad Dog is a last minute desperate defensive tactic to double up on the man with the ball and get possession. The goalie plays as a defender to either help in the double or to cover the crease area.

Pipe: The pipe is the front structure of a metal lacrosse goal frame. It measures six feet by six feet. Players boast of hitting the pipe with shots that are inches away from scoring.

Pole: Pole is slang for a defensive player who uses a long stick measuring from 52 to 72 inches in length.

Short Stick: Short stick is slang for a player using a stick measuring from 40 to 42 inches in length. Attackmen or midfielders play with short sticks.

Slide: The slide is a tactic the defense uses to help defend against a dodger. If the dodger is about to get past the player who is guarding him and is getting near the goal, the other defensive players will slide in—or shift over—to help out. The first slider to help is called the "hot" defender. The "hot" job moves between the six defenders, depending on which one is closest to the ball.

Slow Break: The slow break is an offensive play similar to a fast break but with more players in place for a 5 versus 4 situation. With more defenders in place, the offense usually rotates behind the goal before a shot is taken, if they get to shoot at all.

Stick Hitch: A stick hitch is a ball handling technique used to fake out opponents. The player with the ball makes a subtle fake pass or shot that freezes his opponent (including the goalie for a shooter). Once the opponent has committed in one direction, the player with the ball speeds into open space to either shoot or pass.

Sudden Victory Overtime: If a game is tied after regulation time has run out, sudden victory overtime is an extra four minute period added to decide who will win the game. The first team to score a goal in overtime is the winner, and the game is over immediately, even if there is more time remaining on the clock. If no player scores in four minutes, additional sudden victory overtimes are played until a goal is scored. This overtime used to be called "sudden death."

Tewaaraton Trophy: Tewaaraton is a term for the Mohawk's native game. The Tewaaraton Trophy is the equivalent of football's Heisman trophy. It is given to the top male and female college lacrosse players of the year. It is an enormous honor for the players who receive it, and their teams.

Tom Marechek: Tom Marechek is a Canadian born player and three-time first team All American attackman from Syracuse University. He won championships with the NCAA Orangemen, the NLL Philadephia Wings, the MLL Baltimore/ Washington Bayhawks, and the Canadian World Games teams. He is a legendary lacrosse champion.

Top of the Box: The top of the box is the line twenty yards in front of the goal. It is the top of the large box that is drawn around the goal. Once the offensive team clears the ball across the midfield line, they have 10 seconds to get the ball into the box. If they keep possession of the ball and move out of the box, they must move the ball back into the box within 10 seconds. If the offense fails to get the ball into the box within this time, the opposing team is awarded the turnover. When an offensive player is inside the box, he becomes a threat to the defense. The top of the box is the place that a defensive player picks up the offensive player he will guard.

10-2-WIN

Ten Sport Psychology Techniques You Can Use to Take Your Lacrosse Game From Good to Great

1. Train and Trust

Once you have learned how to do a skill in lacrosse, you need to let your body take over and do what it naturally does, without letting your mind get in the way. **Training** needs to take place in practice and stop during competition. Practice is a good time to be critical of your skills and work on improving your technique—the time to develop mastery of skills. But if you are still in the training mode when you compete, you will lack confidence and worry about making mistakes. Your mind will be focused on the mistakes you don't want to make, and you can actually send messages to your body that will make it do just what you don't want it to do!

Trusting means not worrying about how you are doing the skills anymore once the game begins. During the game, you need to focus on what is happening right that minute. Don't coach yourself or worry about a play you just made; just be fully aware of what is going on in the game, and be ready to respond. Some players call this being present, or being in the moment. If you are a trusting player, you are a confident player. You know that you've practiced and your body will do its best if you don't bother it with a bunch of internal trash talk.

When you develop the ability to train and trust by giving yourself cues that remind you to stay focused, big game situations do not seem so crucial. They become exciting opportunities to pit your best skills against your opponent and truly enjoy playing the game. Playing your best without thinking about it is called being in the zone, and that is where success happens.

2. Set Goals

Your goals are your personal map that leads you to success, the map that shows you how to get where you want to be. No one else's map looks exactly like yours. Your biggest goal is your **dream.** Your lacrosse dream might be making a select team like Max, being a starter, playing in college, or just being a great player. Only you can decide what you want to get out of lacrosse or any other sport.

Pitfalls, doubts, and mistakes can knock you off the path as you travel toward your goals. When you have a dream, it serves as a beacon and steers you back on course when you have setbacks—and there will always be setbacks. In your quest to be a successful lacrosse player, setting goals is the most important place to begin.

Once you have your big dream in place, make small goals to outline the steps you need to take as you work toward the big dream. But be careful not to get too wrapped up in these smaller goals. If you become over concerned about achieving them and lose faith in yourself when you miss one, you will lose sight of the big picture.

It's just like watching the scoreboard during a game or counting strokes during a round of golf. When you are too worried about the results, you are no longer playing in the moment. You certainly aren't in the zone. Keeping score prevents you from trusting. Let the referee worry about the score. When you can stop judging and criticizing yourself and get into the actual process of playing the game, you have the best chance of achieving the score you want. When you are fully focused on playing lacrosse, your goals will eventually take care of themselves.

Break your goals into short-term and long-term goals. Give yourself a different time frame to achieve each one. Decide what skill you want to master first. If you are a defender, focus on picking up ground balls. If you play attack, focus on your shots. Break down mastery of that skill into segments and give yourself a certain amount of time to reach those little goals—for instance you might say, "I am going to do 50 shots on goal every day for two weeks. After two weeks, I want to get 40 out of those 50 shots into the goal."

If you are on a team, you can ask your coach to give you suggestions about which skills might improve your game the most. Coaches love to see players who are motivated to improve.

Set up a personal practice routine that takes you through each of the skills your position requires. The trick is to set your goals and begin working toward them, but don't confuse your small goals with your dream. Once you start working toward any goal, you need to enjoy the work. Remind yourself how good it feels to have a challenge and to be committed to meeting it. Write down your dream and map out the steps you will take to reach it, but then begin to enjoy the journey. Soon enough, you will arrive at your destination.

3. Practice Like You Want to Play

The best way to be ready to perform in a game is to make your practice like a game. Create practices for yourself that take the tactics and skills you need to use in a game and use them in drills that create game-like situations. Lacrosse is made up of a variety of activities that use different combinations of players and areas of the field. Once you master the skill required for a certain activity—for instance, if you're a defender, once you can pick up a ground ball consistently, you need to do drills that use that skill in a game-like way with an opponent and a competitive element.

A team practice should include a range of drills which focus on each type of interaction players will face in a game. You can quickly see that if players don't commit to mastering their individual skills, the team can't even practice efficiently.

The drills that you do individually or with your team can have conditioning (fitness) elements hidden in them, but practice should always have elements of fun. If practice time becomes too long and complicated, it will be very hard for you to stay motivated, you'll get worn down, and you won't enjoy lacrosse. Too much physical preparation can just confuse you, especially if you are new to the game.

But, there are ways to practice mentally that many players overlook, and they can be the difference between good and great performances. And the best thing is, you can practice your mental routines anywhere!

4. Create Mental Routines

You can produce your own mental video about what you want to do in a lacrosse game. Affirming the successful ways you want to play by creating images in your mind and writing down your goals with details will give you an edge in confidence. Here's how you do it: once you've written down your dream performance—you scoring a hat trick, you stealing the ball from your arch-rival, or you dodging around a defender to shoot and score—then imagine what that performance looks like. Once you've gotten the script and the images down, you can watch the movie—starring you—whenever you want. Slowly replay your mental performance, making sure to use specific sports actions in the present tense.

"With both hands on my stick, I fiercely check Johnny's stick and when I knock the ball from his stick, I scoop it up and fast break for the goal. I shoot high-to-low and score!" Make sure to include color imagery—the blue blur you make as you streak down the field—and sound—the fans calling out your name as you score. Just as your dream is a map created by you specifically for you, your movie is all yours. It won't look like anybody else's.

By watching this movie in your mind again and again, you can actually program your mind to accept great performances. Visualizing creates a situation in your brain called "déjà vu." That's just a French way of saying "Wow, I feel like I've been there/done that before." Even if you have never checked Johnny, stolen the ball, and made a fast break to score in real life, if you have done it enough times in your mind, your body won't know the difference! Once you start checking Johnny, your body goes into automatic pilot and says "Here's the part where I steal the ball and score." You have the confidence you need to finish the job, to succeed and not fear the success.

Your mental practice is just as valuable as your skill work, your game-like drills, and your conditioning. Just like you monitor weights and repetitions when you train physically, you need to monitor your thoughts and images regularly. If you catch yourself saying, "Oh no, I'm going to drop the ball," chances are you will send just that message to your body. Make a mental movie of yourself successfully carrying the ball, and when you get possession, immediately turn the dial to Channel Number 1—you starring in your best game yet!

5. Take Care of Fitness and Nutrition

Fitness and nutrition are two areas where you can be a champion, no matter how much natural athletic talent you might have been given. All players can be on the same playing field here, because these are variables that all athletes can control. Your genes are different from anybody else's, but you can create a fitness and nutrition plan that will maximize your endurance, strength, speed, and agility.

Your fitness level will vary from pre-season, in-season, to post season. During your season, you should taper off your conditioning work as a competition gets closer. When you are well fueled and fit, you have a better chance of competing at a higher level than an athlete who is tired and full of junk food.

You can get your workout through practice or you can make it the focus of your training, depending on the situation. When you are just beginning your season, you might need to just get out there and gut it out through a few laps and a barrage of pushups on a regular basis until you have established a fitness base. Once you are "in shape," your muscles will begin to lose the benefits of training after just a few days, so you'll need to consistently challenge yourself to stay fit. You need to be consistent with your fitness and nutrition plans, but also change things up to keep it fresh. If you don't think you can run another lap, run some stairs, swim some laps, or get on your bike.

Cross training is a great way to keep conditioning fresh, and cross training between sports is one of the best ways to stay in shape in the off season. If you play another sport besides lacrosse, you are more likely to be recruited by a college coach. Specializing in just one sport when you are young can make you get tired, bore you, create high expectations in you and your parents and stress you out. If you get stressed about lacrosse it is hard to relax again, and the bad feelings created by the stress can eventually cause you to drop out of the sport you were originally so excited to play.

6. Keep a Positive Focus

Staying in a positive frame of mind will keep you on the path toward success. Making mistakes and having things not go your way are a normal part of playing any sport. None of us are Tom Marechek every day, except Tom Marechek, and even he had bad days on the field.

How you respond to problems is what will determine how well you will perform in the end. When a situation arises in a game or a practice situation, it is very important for you to respond rather than react. Responding means choosing actions that will improve the situation; reacting means letting the situation make you act in a certain way. Responding in a positive way will improve any negative situation and can often turn it into an opportunity. It's natural to be disappointed when things don't go your way, but don't let it freak you out.

Dwelling on problems while you play will focus you on negative events. We all drop the ball some times. If you continue to focus on your mistakes, you will eventually make those thoughts part of your reality—a situation that is known as a self-fulfilling prophecy. The game will just pass you by.

When you have confidence and are playing in the present moment, you don't give those routine errors too much thought. Brush off those dropped balls or even missed goals. Flush them out of your mind with positive thoughts and keep in tune with the ongoing game. When you choose to think about the things you do well and have fun playing the game, you can quickly replace the feeling of failure when you make a mistake with the refusal to be affected by your mistakes.

Treat yourself with the same understanding that you would your best friend, and your mistakes will suddenly seem like a normal part of the game—not a burden that drags you down. Letting go of your mistakes can keep you from falling apart—physically and mentally. Don't let anyone make you feel like you need to keep reliving a mistake—that is not good for your game or your team.

7. Relax

To maximize your performance, it is very important to get plenty of rest and relaxation. The two are similar, but not the same, and both are important. Rest means getting plenty of sleep and not exhausting your body with over-training. Rest helps build and heal muscle fibers and gives your body the chance to recover from practice and be ready for competition.

Relaxation means resting your mind from worrying about any one thing too much—lacrosse, a game, your schoolwork, anything that you are concerned about. Relaxation clears your mind for better visualization routines. There are many ways to relax. Learning proper breathing techniques is important for calming your nerves in clutch situations.

If you start to pay attention to your breath, you may find that when you are getting stressed out you take little shallow breaths, just getting air into the top of your lungs. There are a lot of scientific reasons why this type of breathing actually makes you more stressed, but all you need to know is that if you catch yourself breathing like that, stop. Take slow deep breaths that fill your lungs. Relaxed breathing can actually make your mind relax!

Yoga and stretching can increase your flexibility and help you develop physical and mental cues that will remind you to relax during a game. A tight muscle does not have as much strength and flexibility as a muscle that is relaxed. Giving yourself a calming cue is the first step toward being in the moment, the place where peak performances occur.

8. Be a Team Player

Nobody has ever made it to the top of anything all by themself. Success in individual sports still requires a sense of team—whether it is the pit crew of the Grand Prix driver or the caddie of the Open Champion. Although we often see professional athletes mouthing off about how great they are and trash-talking their opponents, you will notice that the true greats of sports have a humble attitude. Humility doesn't mean that you don't acknowledge your talent and hard work; it means you let it speak for itself. Having a quiet confidence and a true appreciation of the role that every member of your team plays in being successful will make other people want to work with you and can help you reach your individual dream.

Being a team player means trusting your teammates, as well. Individual effort and performance is required for team success, but teams only win when players work together for the team, not for themselves. How many truly gifted players have you seen who never made it to the Hall of Fame in their sport because their team never won a national championship?

You need to do the best job you possibly can at your position, and trust your teammates to do the same. Trusting your teammates also takes pressure off of you. When you are supportive of the other players on your team, you will help them to be in the zone and play the best game they are able to play. No one has ever gotten a better performance from anyone by shaming him. Help your teammates to brush off their inevitable mistakes and move forward, the same way you do for yourself. Great teammates compete against each other in practice and complete each other in games.

9. Make Your Core Values Your Lifestyle

Other people can derail you from your quest for success—sometimes they don't mean to get in your way, and sometimes they do. If you have a non-negotiable set of core values in place, choices are easier to make.

Core values are the ways you have decided to live your life to reach your dream. Your core values are as unique as your dream and the map you create to reach it. Core values can be any promise you make to yourself: *I will practice ground balls twenty minutes at home every day; I will get eight hours of sleep every night; I will learn from players that I respect by making time to watch them on television, read about them in the newspaper and go to their games whenever possible; I will spend one night every weekend with my family so I can keep my perspective; I will get my homework done early every night so I can keep my grades up and stay on the team; I will read every night from a book about a great lacrosse player; I will spend ten minutes every morning going through the mental movie of my success before I get out of bed.* The possibilities are endless. Non-negotiable means you are doing it—no matter what. You won't let people talk you out of it.

You can use your core values on big and little levels: If your friend really wants you to go to a movie instead of practicing, remind yourself that your friend does not have the map toward your dream. Set up a time to go to the movie with him that doesn't take you away from your quest. If someone you hang out with wants you to do something bad for your health, like trying cigarettes, and one of your core values is keeping your body as fit as possible, you can just say "No, I need to keep in shape." "No" is easier to say when you have your core values—your unique pillars of power—in place.

Your core values give you the mental strength to be in charge of the way you live your life, instead of letting your friends, TV, or the Internet tell you who to be.

10. Be Confident

Do you believe you have the ability to get the job done on the field? Confidence is the most important thing you can carry with you into a lacrosse game. Sometimes it seems that certain people are just born confident, or they have so much natural ability that they deserve to be confident. But, no matter what your physical gifts are, you can build your confidence.

The first nine 10-2-Win principles are the steps to follow to develop your ability to believe in yourself and be the best possible lacrosse player you can be. Each one is important, and you should make them the foundation of your experience in any sport. *Train, then trust and free it up. Set goals to aim toward your dream. Practice like you want to play in games. Mentally rehearse positive plays and performances. Be physically fit. Keep your thoughts positive. Stay relaxed. Be a team player and trust your teammates. Hold tight to your core values when you make choices.* When you practice these principles regularly, you will become more confident.

When you are a confident athlete, you will have fun just playing lacrosse. You are not playing for the sake of winning every outing—you enjoy meeting the challenges that come up as you move toward your dream.

You are a successful athlete, with or without a scoreboard.

For more sport psychology techniques that you can apply to lacrosse and your other favorite sports, check out *www.trainandtrust.com.*